Judi Wiegman

Beacon Hill Press of Kansas City
Kansas City, Missouri

Copyright 2004
by Beacon Hill Press of Kansas City

Printed in the United States of America

ISBN 083-412-0895

Cover Design: Darlene Filley/Jeremy Dale
Illustrator: Jeremy Dale

Editor: Donna Manning
Assistant Editor: Stephanie Harris

Note: This story is based on factual information about missionaries. It is part of the *Understanding Christian Mission,* Children's Mission Education curriculum. It is designed to correlate with this year's theme, The Missionary. Lessons focus on the call, preparation, life, and work of career missionaries.

Dedication

To my missionary friends Rueben and Monica Fernandez and their sons, Juan and Andres, who inspired the story for this book. Reuben is the Rector of Seminario Nazareneo de las Americas in San Jose, Costa Rica.

Contents

1

The News

"Mom! Dad!" Brian shouted as he rushed in the door. "I made the soccer team! This is the best day of my life!"

Brian stopped in his tracks. His parents were sitting on the couch. Their pastor was praying with them. Brian thought something terrible had happened.

Mom stood up and gave Brian a hug. "I'm really proud of you!"

Dad joined the hug. "That's great news, Brian. Way to go! You've worked very hard."

"I'm certainly glad I came," Pastor Thomas said as he walked toward the door. "This house is full of good news today."

"Brian, sit here beside me," Dad instructed. "We have something to tell you. It's about our call to be missionaries. You know we've filled out papers and made trips to Kansas City to meet with church leaders. We've been waiting a long time for an answer."

Brian nodded as they all sat down.

Dad continued. "Your mother and I asked Pastor Thomas to come and pray with us today because we received an important call from Nazarene International Headquarters in Kansas City. We've been assigned to serve in Costa Rica. I'll be teaching at the seminary [SEM-uh-nair-ee] where people, such as pastors and missionaries, are trained for ministry. But there's a lot to be done before we leave. This is a great day for our family!"

Filled with disappointment, Brian bit his lower lip. Then he shouted, "It's not fair! Why now? I just made the All-Star Soccer team! I can't leave now!" He bolted from the couch and ran down the hall to his room.

Brian flopped down on the edge of his bed. "I worked so hard this year to make the team," he mumbled as he kicked his soccer ball across the room. "And what about my friends?"

Just then he heard a knock at the door. It was his mom. "Come in," he managed to say.

"Brian," she began, "we aren't leaving tomorrow, you know."

"I'm sorry, Mom," he replied. "I guess I just wasn't expecting to hear the news right now. I know we've been praying for this, and I should be excited. But I-I . . ." Brian buried his face in the pillow. Mom stayed for a few minutes and then left him alone in his room. She knew he needed some time to be alone.

Brian turned over and stared at the ceiling. "Dear God," he prayed, "I know You want our family to go to Costa Rica. But I didn't think it would be this soon. Please help me. Amen."

There was a gentle tap on the door. "Brian," Mom said, "supper's ready. Wash up and come on."

"I'm coming, Mom," he replied. Brian washed his hands and face and joined his family at the table.

"Let's pray," Dad said as he bowed his head. "Father, we thank You for our food today. Please help us prepare to serve You as missionaries. Amen."

When Brian looked up, his parents were smiling.

"Brian," Dad said, "we're very proud of you." He winked as he continued, "I hope to see several of those soccer games before we leave Texas."

Suddenly Brian had to choke back his tears. This was the worst day of his life.

2

Summer Camp

The doors on the vans burst open. Campers poured out to greet each other and get reacquainted. They had arrived for a fun-filled week at Camp Arrowhead, the West Texas District Campground.

The boys ran straight toward the Brazos [BRAH-zohs] River. Every year they checked out the water level, hoping they would get to go tubing on the river or hiking along its banks.

"Hey, Brian!" Trent shouted as he saw him coming down the trail. "Check out the river!"

"Hey, man! That's way cool!" Brian gave Trent a high five. "Looks like we're going to have fun this week." Brian was excited about spending time with his friends. He hoped it would help him forget about Costa Rica for a few days.

The boys headed back toward the vans to collect their belongings. After dragging their stuff to the dorm and making up their bunks, they were hot and sweaty.

11

Suddenly James, one of Brian's cabin mates, shouted, "Water balloons!"

The boys leaped from their bunks and headed to the outside faucet. Blasting each other with water balloons felt good.

Their play was interrupted by the bell. The boys knew they had 10 minutes to clean up and report to the chapel. It was time for the director to review camp rules and daily schedules.

"Activities this year include water games, the climbing wall, archery, crafts, and video time," said the director. Then he gave us the best news of all. "Campers," he began, "the river is perfect this year. So we will all get to ride the tubes to the cookout site on Thursday night."

Shouts of joy rang throughout the chapel.

The director continued, "Some of the activities are electives. That means you can choose which activities you want to participate in. Others, such as Mission Mania, are required."

Brian groaned because he knew that meant EVERYONE had to go!

Then the director introduced the camp

workers. Among them was Miss Judi, who would teach Mission Mania. She was carrying a gun that sprayed bubbles. The kids around her tried to catch the bubbles as she sprayed them in the air. Brian tried to ignore her. He was glad when they were dismissed for supper.

The first full day at camp was going fast. It was time for Brian's team to go to Mission Mania. Miss Judi told the counselors they could take a break and leave the boys with her and her assistant.

"All 50 of them?" one counselor questioned.

"Are you sure?" another one asked. "I hope they pay attention."

"I'm sure they will," Miss Judi chuckled. "Learning about missions CAN be fun."

But Brian wasn't so sure.

3

CURIOS and QUESTIONS

Brian stared at the decorations around the room. Colorful, inflatable worlds, the size of large beach balls, were spinning gently as they hung from the ceiling. There were tables full of unusual items from all over the world. Miss Judi called them curios [KYUR-ee-ohs].

"Who can tell me what a missionary does?" Miss Judi asked.

"A missionary goes to another culture to tell people about Jesus," came the reply.

"Good answer!" Miss Judi asked another question. "Do missionaries get paid?"

"No!" everyone responded.

"Well now," Miss Judi said as she looked directly at Brian, "suppose you were on the mission field with your family, and you needed new shoes. If your dad didn't get paid, how would you buy them?"

When Brian didn't answer, Miss Judi continued. "During the next few days, we're going to learn the answers to these and other questions about missionaries. I'm excited to have you in this class. Is there anyone here who has a missionary in their family?"

Brian raised his hand. He wasn't sure he wanted to admit it. "My parents and I are going to Costa Rica soon."

Several kids said, "Wow!"

"We're proud to have you with us, Brian. We'll pray for you and your family every day. Can anyone tell me where Costa Rica is located?" Miss Judi unrolled a big world map.

"It's in Central America," someone answered.

"That's right," Miss Judi said as she pointed to it on the map. "Costa Rica is warm all year long. And the country is very beautiful. There are lots of flowers, colorful birds, and even monkeys."

"Miss Judi, I know something that's made in Costa Rica," James said.

"What's that?" Miss Judi questioned.

"Computer chips!" he exclaimed. "Costa Rica makes the chips and sends them to other countries. My dad works for a computer company, and he told me."

"Thank you, James. That's interesting. Costa Rica also sells lots of coffee and bananas to other countries," added Miss Judi.

She looked at Brian and smiled. "I hope you like soccer, Brian. It's the national sport in Costa Rica."

A smile crept across Brian's face.

"Guys, we need to pray for Brian's family. God has called his parents to be missionaries. And Brian will be an MK—a missionary kid. Let's pray for them now."

4

MORE QUESTIONS

"Now let's talk money!" Miss Judi exclaimed. "How do missionaries get paid? That's the next question. Some of your parents may be doctors, store clerks, lawyers, or factory workers. They get paid for the work they do. God calls some people to work as missionaries. They may preach, work in offices and hospitals, or teach in schools. They also get paid for their work. How do you think they get paid?"

"I know," said Trent, raising his hand. "Offerings."

"That's a good answer," Miss Judi replied.

Brian gave Trent another high five.

Miss Judi explained. "The Church of the Nazarene has a wonderful way of caring for our missionaries. Have any of you heard of the World Evangelism Fund?"

"I have," said a boy named Michael. "My mom is the missionary president at our church. People give offerings to this fund every year."

"That's right," said Miss Judi. "Churches then send the money to our Nazarene Headquarters in Kansas City. Each missionary receives money from this fund to help meet their needs while they serve on the mission field. So when Brian goes to Costa Rica, each of your churches will help care for his family."

Everyone smiled at Brian. Brian was smiling too.

Miss Judi told the campers many interesting facts. She taught them that the Church of the Nazarene divides the world into seven regions—Eurasia, Mexico and Central America, South America, the Caribbean, Africa, Asia-Pacific, and the United States and Canada. She had everyone play games to help them remember these regions.

Miss Judi explained that there are missionaries in each of the seven regions. The class was surprised to learn not all missionaries are sent to other cultures from the United States. Some are sent from other regions to be Nazarene missionaries.

The campers enjoyed reading the missionary books that Miss Judi brought with her. They read them during rest time and then traded with

each other. Some counselors read them to the campers before "lights out."

Camp was coming to a close. During the last chapel service, the camp speaker, Pastor Mike, asked, "Has God spoken to anyone this week about serving Him? Has He called you to serve Him as a missionary? Maybe God's voice spoke to you while you were with Miss Judi. If so, I invite you to come and kneel at the altar."

Brian went forward. He knew God had spoken to him this week. There were seven at the altar, including a counselor! Miss Judi prayed with each person.

Camp was over. Brian said good-bye to his friends while they loaded the vans.

As they headed home, Brian looked out the window. He wondered if he would ever return to Camp Arrowhead.

5

Ready to Go!

Brian could hardly wait to see his parents and tell them what happened. He ran from the van to meet them.

"I have the best news! You should have been there. Seven of us prayed about serving God on the mission field. But I get to go sooner than the rest of them!"

Brian's parents hugged him. They were pleased and relieved. They had sent an unhappy boy to camp, but he returned happy and excited. Their prayers had been answered.

Brian burst into his room to find suitcases and lots of boxes. "What's going on here?" he asked as he dumped his camp stuff on the bed.

"We're packing our suitcases to go to Kansas City for a few months," Dad explained. "Your mom and I must complete the training for our mission assignment. We're packing these boxes to put in crates that will be sent on to Costa Rica. We want them to be there when we arrive."

Brian glanced around his room. He would need to sort through everything and decide what to take to Kansas City and what to pack for Costa Rica.

A phone call interrupted Brian's thoughts. It was his friend Levi inviting him to join the guys for laser tag and hamburgers. He quickly shifted his thoughts from packing to having fun with the guys. This was just what he needed.

Levi's dad soon arrived to pick up Brian.

"Hey, Brian, what's up?" Levi asked. "My mom says you're moving to Kansas City for a few months. Is that true?"

"Yeah, we'll be leaving soon," Brian replied.

"This is way cool!" exclaimed Levi. "My parents go there a lot on business. Maybe I can come and hang out with you."

Brian grinned. "No kidding?" He put his arm around Levi's neck as they headed toward the car. "Man, am I glad to hear that. Maybe you can hang out a whole week!"

* * *

While his parents completed their missionary training in Kansas City, Brian attended school and played indoor soccer with a church team. In a few weeks they would leave for Costa Rica. But first, they would return to Texas and spend the Christmas holidays with their family and friends. Brian couldn't wait to see everyone!

✳ ✳ ✳

The time in Texas passed quickly. Brian became more excited about the adventure they were about to begin. Friends and family were eager to know about their plans.

When school restarted, Brian went to say good-bye to his friends. He found them crowded around a bulletin board in the hall. They were talking excitedly about something.

"What's up?" Brian asked as he tried to get a look.

"Er, uh," Levi stuttered, "uh, the January soccer schedule is posted."

Brian stared at the bulletin board. Every year his name had been on this list. But this time, it was missing.

6

New Worlds to Conquer!

As their jet landed on the runway in San Jose, the capital city of Costa Rica, Brian wondered what it would be like. When they left Dallas, it was winter. But when he stepped from the plane, he realized it was very hot.

On their way to the seminary, Brian saw lots of bright-colored flowers everywhere. And there were adobe [uh-DOH-bee] houses with brightly painted roofs. Brian remembered the discussion at camp. "Miss Judi was right," he thought. "Costa Rica is just like she told us."

Brian was excited when they arrived at their house. They found the crates they had sent months earlier.

Brian dumped his backpack on the floor and ran outside to explore. Suddenly he heard the sound of voices cheering and shouting. When he reached the sound, he could hardly believe his eyes. There it was! A beautiful, green soccer field!

"Mom! Dad!" he shouted as he ran back to the house. "You aren't going to believe this! Where's my stuff? Help me find my soccer ball!" The excitement in his voice brought his dad immediately.

"Whoa," Dad said. "What's up, Brian? Why do you need your soccer ball?"

"You aren't going to believe this!" Brian exclaimed. "Right outside, over there . . ." Brian motioned as he began digging through a box. "Soccer! They're playing soccer!"

"Looking for this?" Mom walked into the room and tossed Brian's favorite soccer ball to him.

"Way to go, Mom!" he shouted as he ran out the door.

Brian stopped near the edge of the field and sat down on his soccer ball.

"Hi," a voice from behind him called. "Are you Brian?"

Brian stood up to see a boy his age smiling at him. "Yes, my name is Brian. How do you know?" he asked.

"My name is Andres [AHN-drays]," he

replied. "My dad is Rueben Fernandez, president of the seminary. My brother Juan [Wahn] and I have been waiting for you to get here."

Andres pointed to a boy on the field. "That's Juan. I'll introduce you to him. Hey, Juan!" Andres shouted. "Brian's here. Come and meet him."

"Pleased to meet you," Juan said as he shook Brian's hand. "I hear you love to play soccer."

"I sure do," Brian replied.

"Come on." Andres motioned. "Meet our friends and join us."

The three boys walked across the field together. This was the best day of Brian's life.